COOL COMPUTING JOBS

# WEB DESIGN

NANCY DICKMANN

Published in 2024 by
**KidHaven Publishing, an Imprint of Greenhaven Publishing, LLC**
2544 Clinton St., Buffalo, NY 14224



Text and Editor: Nancy Dickmann
Children's Publisher: Anne O'Daly
Design Manager: Keith Davis
Designer and Illustrator: Supriya Sahai
Picture Manager: Sophie Mortimer

Picture Credits
Key: t=top, b=bottom, c=center, l=left, r=right
Interior:Shutterstock: Mongkolchon Akesin 8; asharkuy 5, 29b; Yaroslav Astakhov 23; Chaosamran_Studio 13, 28; DC Studio 14; drserg 6; fizkes 4, 9; fotoinfot 22; Elizaveta Galitckaia 12; galsand 20; Gorodenkoff 25; Industry Views 24; Insta photos 26; Anna Jurkovska 18; Lucky Business 11; PK Studio 7; Rawpixel.com 10; REDPIXEL.PL 16; sdecoret 19; Melody Smart 15; Max Thanathip 21; Tero Vesalainen 17, 29t; Drazen Zigic 27.

**Cataloging-in-Publication Data**

Names: Dickmann, Nancy.
Title: Web design / Nancy Dickmann.
Description: Buffalo, New York: KidHaven Publishing, 2024. | Series: Cool computing jobs | Includes glossary and index.
Identifiers: ISBN 9781534546592 (pbk.) | ISBN 9781534546608 (library bound) | ISBN 9781534546615 (ebook)
Subjects: LCSH: Web sites--Design--Juvenile literature. | Web site development--Vocational guidance--Juvenile literature. | Web sites--Design--Vocational guidance--Juvenile literature.
Classification: LCC TK5105.888 D534 2024 | DDC 006.7--dc23



Manufactured in the United States of America

CPSIA compliance information: Batch #CW24KH: For further information contact Greenhaven Publishing LLC at 1-844-317-7404.

Please visit our website, www.greenhavenpublishing.com.
For a free color catalog of all our high-quality books, call toll free 1-844-317-7404 or fax 1-844-317-7405.

Find us on

# CONTENTS

# AN ONLINE WORLD

**The internet is amazing. We can do so many things online!**

We use the internet to do many things! Maybe you've watched videos or researched a school report online. Adults might shop, order food, or buy plane tickets online. These online activities often happen through websites. Websites display information and allow us to interact with it online.

**Many people use websites to catch up on the latest news.**

## What Does It Mean?

"Online" means "connected to a worldwide network of computers." They are connected in a way that lets them "talk" to each other. Some are connected by wires. Others are connected wirelessly. They send and receive signals from antennas and satellites.

There are cables under the oceans that stretch for thousands of miles to connect computers.

Many computers are connected by fiber-optic cables, made from thin strands of glass.

# WEBSITES

**Sometimes it's hard to remember that websites are still pretty new.**

Tim Berners-Lee is often credited as the inventor of the World Wide Web. He's a computer scientist.

The world's first website launched in 1991. Five years later, there were 2 million websites. Today, there are more than 1 billion! They look very different from the earliest websites. Those were mainly just text. They had simple graphics, but no videos or animation.

There is a lot of information on the web! Search engines like Google help you find what you need.

## Modern Websites

Today's websites often have photos, videos, and animated graphics. Some let you choose items and put them in a digital shopping basket. Others let you search for information within the site. Icons let you share to social media with a single click.

The internet is the network of computers that allows us to access the web.

01

# LEADING THE TEAM

**Many people who want to have a website don't make it themselves.**

Most companies have websites. Bands and politicians do too. They often hire a web development team to build the website. They describe what they want the website to do. They share their ideas about what it will look like. Then, the development team turns the ideas into reality.

**The person or organization that hires a web development team is called the client.**

## Project Managers

A project manager leads the team. They talk to the client about their needs. They assign jobs to the team members. A project manager is in charge of schedules and budgets. They keep the team organized. Their job is to make sure the project runs smoothly.

Project managers need to understand how websites are built so they can give the client advice on what's possible.

A project manager needs good communication and leadership skills.

# DESIGNING A LOOK

**Every website has its own look. Getting it right is important!**

Some websites are sleek and elegant. Others are bright and colorful. The look tells you about the company or person whose website it is. A web designer is in charge of planning a website's look. They choose colors and a design style.

A person who does this job is sometimes also called a graphic designer.

## Skills

A web designer needs to be creative and good at art. They might sketch things out by hand, then use computer drawing tools to make a finished version. They also need to understand computers so they know what will work on a website.

There are different software programs to help web designers. Figma is one of the most popular design programs.

A web designer will show their sketches to the client to get feedback.

# FINDING YOUR WAY

**Even the simplest websites need to be well organized. Otherwise users can't find what they need!**

UX designers plan the basic structure that a website is built on, which is like its skeleton.

A website is a collection of different pages. They are all linked together. You can use menus or click buttons to move from one page to another. The UX designer plans how the different pages will be arranged. These letters stand for "user experience." The UX designer wants to make a website easy to use.

Wireframes have no pictures and very little color.

A wireframe makes it easy to make changes before the website is coded.

## Wireframe

The UX designer makes a wireframe to show how the website will fit together. The wireframe doesn't have the final text or fancy graphics. It's more like a framework for the website. It shows how the pages link together and where the menus will be.

# SPEAKING THEIR LANGUAGE

**Coding happens after the website is planned.**

Computers don't speak English or Spanish. They communicate in ones and zeroes. We use programming languages to give computers instructions. There are many different languages. Each one has its own terms and symbols. The computer translates them into ones and zeroes.

Many web developers are able to use several different programming languages.

## Languages for Web Design

Many website coders use a system called HTML. It controls how text and graphics appear on a website. It also creates hyperlinks. CSS is another language that styles text and buttons and makes web pages look good. JavaScript helps add sound, video, and animations.

Computer coding has to be just right. Even a tiny error means that the code won't work.

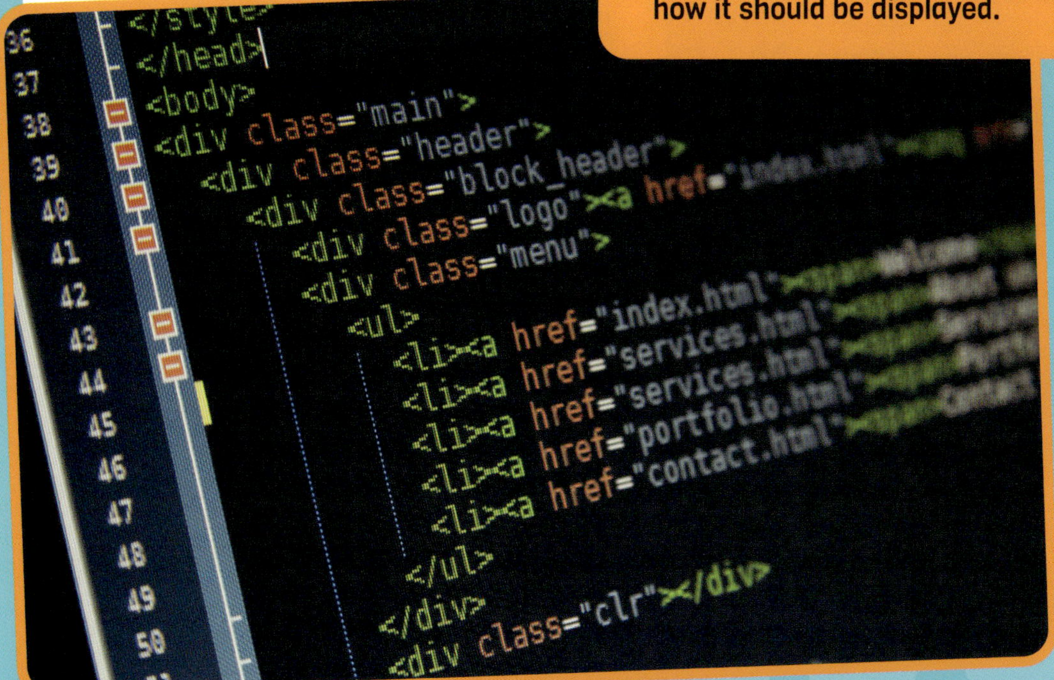


HTML adds tags to text that show how it should be displayed.

# WEB DEVELOPERS

**Web developers and programmers both know how to code to create websites.**

A programmer take the plans and ideas and uses code to turn them into a working website. They write lines of code that will be displayed as a finished page. A web developer can also use coding skills to create a website. They are often involved in the design and planning too.

**Web developers can build entire websites from what looks like lines of text on a screen!**

## At the Front

Many web developers are what's called "front-end developers." They work on the parts of a website that users see. They make sure the text is easy to read and the page layout is working well. They code menus, buttons, and hyperlinks to make the website easy to use.

Front-end developers also work on existing websites, updating them and adding new features.

Buttons can be coded to be tapped with a finger or clicked with a mouse.

01

# THE BACK END

**ALL websites have a lot going on behind the scenes!**

A lot of work happens behind the scenes of a performance. The same is true for websites!

Have you ever been in a play? The audience sees a polished performance, but a lot of work goes on backstage to make this happen. It's the same with a website. A lot of the code doesn't affect how the website looks, but this code makes the website work.

Websites are hosted on banks of servers that connect them to computers all over the world.

## Making It Work

A backend developer is in charge of the parts of the website that users don't see. They make sure it can cope with lots of traffic. They write code to keep it secure. Backend developers use different programming languages. Their code runs on a server to create the webpage.

Shopping websites have to be very secure to keep shoppers' payment details safe.

# FULL STACK DEVELOPERS

**Some web developers can do it all!**

Just like a full stack of pancakes can be all the breakfast you need, a full stack developer can do all the coding!

Front-end and backend developers often use different programming languages. Most developers specialize in one or the other. However, some developers do both. They are known as full stack developers. For small businesses, hiring one can save money.

Puzzles and games are a good way to build problem-solving skills.

## Solving Problems

It takes a lot of experience to become a full stack developer. They have to know many different programming languages. They need to understand how servers and databases work. Full stack developers are good at problem solving. They come up with creative solutions to make great websites.

A good full stack developer has the technical skills to build an entire website from scratch.

# NUTS AND BOLTS

**What do buildings and websites have in common? They both need an architect!**

An architect designs buildings. They make sure the buildings are strong and stable. They also think about how the building will be laid out and what it will look like on the outside. A web architect has a similar role, but they work with computer code instead of blueprints.

An architect draws up a plan for a building that the contractors will follow.

## Web Architects

On a website for buying plane tickets, users want to see what flights are available and the prices of those flights. The website's information needs to be constantly updated as other people buy tickets. A web architect plans how this will work.

A web architect makes sure that the website works on different browsers and devices.

A well-designed website can make it easy to find and buy flights for a vacation.

# TEST IT OUT!

**A web development team needs to make sure a website is working before it launches.**

While a website is being built, the public can't see it. It only goes live once it's ready. Before this happens, it must be tested. A quality assurance (QA) tester looks for any bugs. They report problems to the developers so they can be fixed.

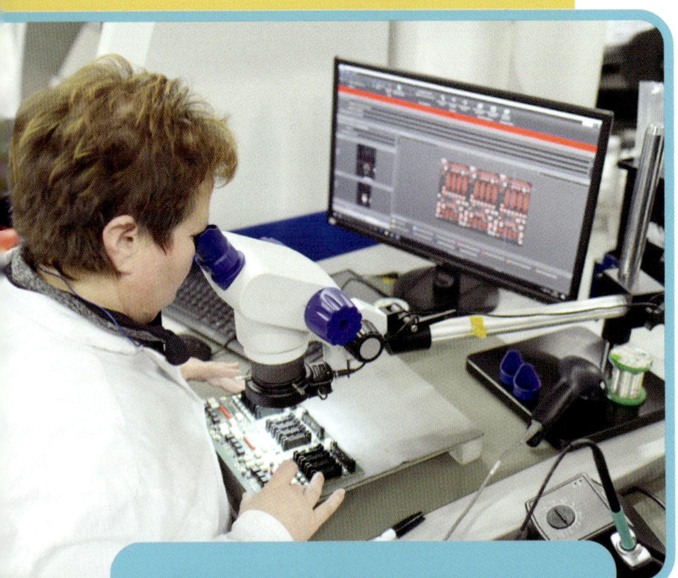

There are also QA testers at work in factories. They test products for any defects.

A QA tester works with the development team. They think of ways to fix any problems.

## Eye for Detail

A QA tester can't just click randomly through the website. This wouldn't find all the problems. They need to be careful and methodical. It's important to test every part of the website. Some QA engineers write software that helps them test the website.

Some web developers test their sites on real users. This shows if they find the site easy to use.

# HOW TO PREPARE

**Web development can be a great career. It's never too early to start!**

Many people who work in web development have a degree in computer science. Others learned on the job. You don't need to wait for college to start learning! Coding is fun and easy to learn. You can try out programming languages that web developers use.

HTML is fairly simple and easy to learn. There are online courses that can help you.

## Try It Out!

Anyone can build a website. There are templates available that do most of the coding for you. Why not try building your own? Think about how people will use it. What features does it need? What do you want it to look like? What will the structure be like?

Online tools such as Wix, Squarespace, and WordPress provide templates that help build websites without coding.

Web development is often done as a team. Working with friends can be fun!

# QUIZ

**Which job in web development is the best fit for you? Answer these questions, and check your results at the end.**

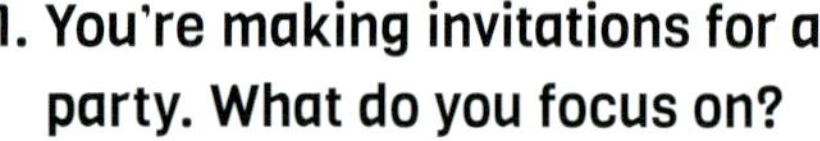

**1. You're making invitations for a party. What do you focus on?**

A. making sure I get the date and time correct

B. choosing the colors and the layout

C. putting the information in a format that's easy to understand

**2. How do you spend your allowance?**

A. I make a strict budget and stick to it.

B. I'm saving up for a new piece of drawing software.

C. I buy boxes and trays to organize my room.

**3. What's your least favorite thing about going on vacation?**

A. having no schedule for the day

B. being away from my art supplies

C. not knowing exactly how to get around

**4. If you and your friends were going to start a band, what would your role be?**

A. planning rehearsals and organizing gigs

B. designing our logo

C. making sure all our equipment is set up to work together

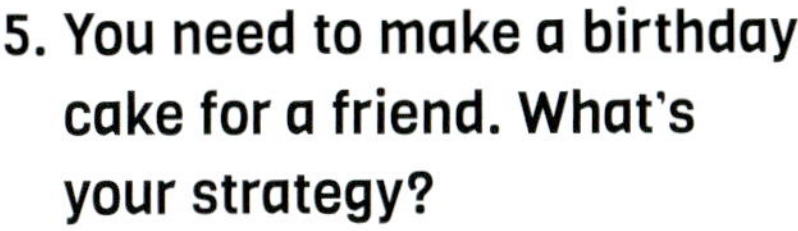

**5. You need to make a birthday cake for a friend. What's your strategy?**

A. find a recipe, make a shopping list, and make sure it's ready on time

B. choose the color scheme first

C. talk to your friend to get a clear idea about what they want their cake to look and taste like

**Add up your answers.**

**What did you get?**

Mostly As: You could be a project manager. You're organized and have leadership skills, and you're good with schedules and budgets.

Mostly Bs: You could be a web designer. You have a creative streak and are interested in making attractive designs.

Mostly Cs: You could be a UX designer. You like things to be clear and organized, and you understand how important it is to have a solid framework.

# GLOSSARY

**budget** a plan setting out how much money is available and how it will be spent

**bug** an error in a computer program or system

**client** a person or organization that hires another company or a freelancer to complete a project for them

**code** a system of letters, numbers, and symbols used as instructions for a computer

**database** a large collection of data that is stored on a computer so it can be used or added to

**digital** done electronically

**factory** a building where products are manufactured

**graphics** pictures and other information displayed on a monitor

**hyperlink** a link on a website that is programmed to take you to a different page if you click on it

**icon** a symbol that represents a computer application on a screen

**program** a set of coded instructions for a computer to follow

**satellites** robotic spacecraft that orbit Earth; some of them transmit signals for computers and phones

**server** a computer that stores and sends out information to other computers

**software** programs for a computer

**template** an electronic file with a predesigned format and structure, ready to be filled in

**wireframe** a very basic version of a website that shows how its menus, buttons, and screens are linked

# FIND OUT MORE

## Books

**Anniss, Matthew.** *Create Your Own Web Site or Blog.* Mankato, MN: Heinemann-Raintree, 2017.

**Hudak, Heather C.** *Dynamic Website Developers.* Minneapolis, MN: Checkerboard Library, 2019.

**Leigh, Anna.** *Design and Build Your Own Website.* Minneapolis, MN: Lerner Publishing, 2020.

**Preuitt, Sheela.** *Mission JavaScript.* Minneapolis, MN: Lerner Publishing, 2020.

**Whitney, David.** *Get Coding 2! Build Five Computer Games Using HTML and JavaScript.* Somerville, MA: Candlewick Press, 2019.

## Websites

Learn more amazing facts about web design here:
**kids.kiddle.co/Web_design**

Go here to find interesting facts about the internet:
**www.sciencekids.co.nz/sciencefacts/technology/internet.html**

Learn more details about computer programming here:
**www.dkfindout.com/uk/computer-coding/**

This website has free online coding courses and activities:
**studio.code.org/courses**

This video explains more about debugging:
**www.bbc.com/bitesize/articles/ztkx6sg**

**Publisher's note to educators and parents: Our editors have carefully reviewed these websites to ensure that they are suitable for students. Many websites change frequently, however, and we cannot guarantee that a site's future contents will continue to meet our high standards of quality and educational value. Be advised that students should be closely supervised whenever they access the internet.**

# INDEX